LIVING IN CASTLE TIMES

Robyn Gee
Illustrated by Rob McCaig
and Iain Ashman
History adviser: Dr Anne Millard

Contents

rst published in 1982 by Usborne Publishing Ltd, Usborne House, 83-85 Saffron Hill,
ndon EC1N 8RT, England
 Printed in Belgium

Thomas and his town

This is Thomas Middleton. He is nine years old. In this book you can find out all about Thomas and his family. They lived about 600 years ago. The big picture shows you the town where they lived.

Lord John lives at the castle. He owns most of the land outside the town walls.

People practise archery in this open space.

There are four gates in the wall. This is one of them. Strangers have to pay to come through them. They are guarded all the time and locked up at night.

In Thomas's time life was very different from nowadays. Here are some of the things that were different:

* There were no cars, lorries, buses, trains or bicycles. People used horses, carriages and carts instead.

* There were no televisions, radios, telephones or newspapers and hardly any books. Messengers carried letters and town criers shouted out the latest news.

* People had no electricity or gas for lights, cooking and heating. They used open fires, candles and lamps.

* There was no running water in the houses. People had to fetch it from wells and rivers. Most people did not have baths or wash very often and most things were much dirtier and smellier than they are now.

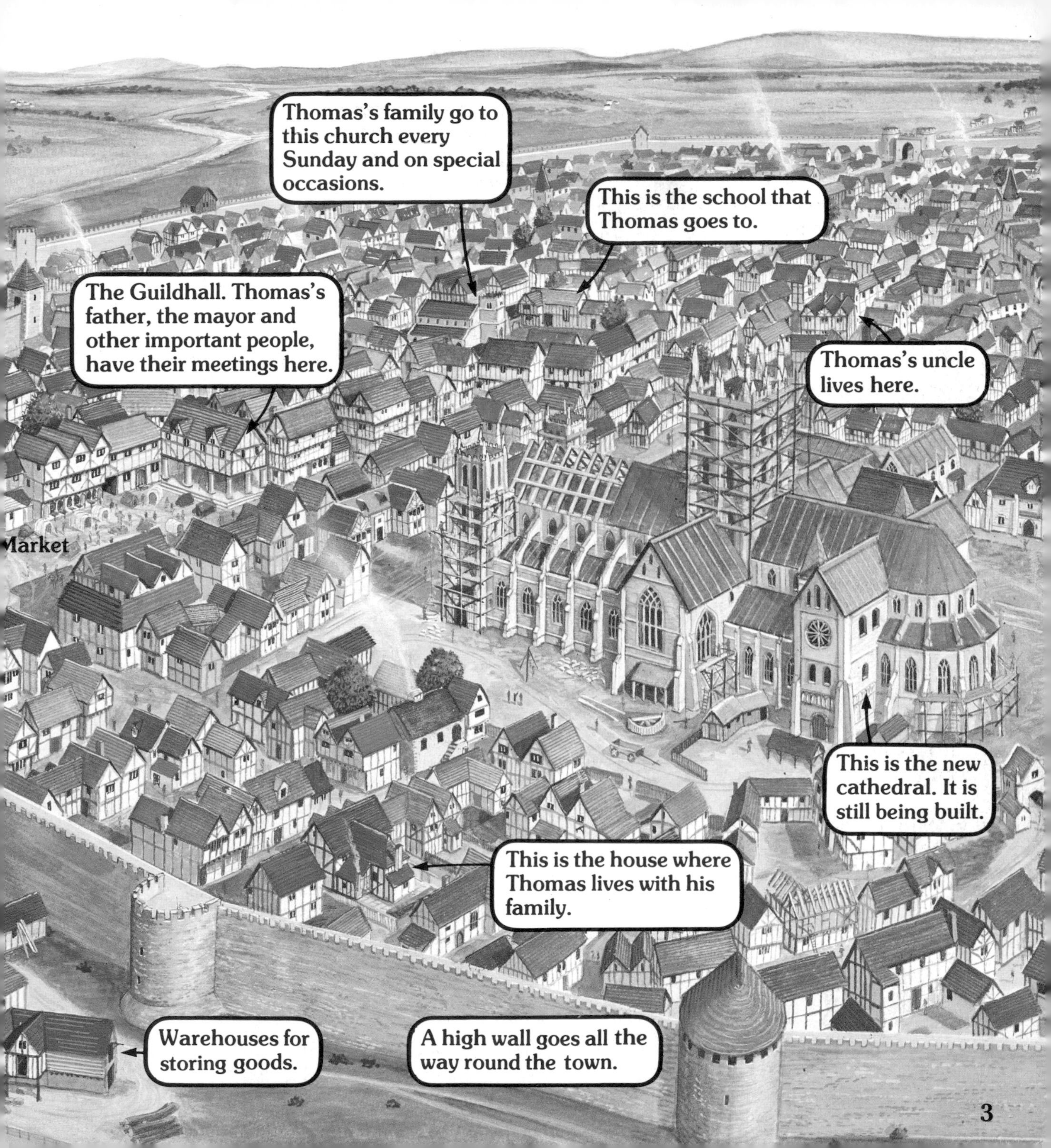
Thomas's family go to this church every Sunday and on special occasions.
This is the school that Thomas goes to.
The Guildhall. Thomas's father, the mayor and other important people, have their meetings here.
Thomas's uncle lives here.
Market
This is the new cathedral. It is still being built.
This is the house where Thomas lives with his family.
Warehouses for storing goods.
A high wall goes all the way round the town.

Thomas's house and family

Here are the people in Thomas's family.

Thomas's father, Master Middleton, is a goldsmith. His mother, Mistress Middleton, is always busy with the jobs that need doing around the house.

Thomas has one brother and one sister. His brother, Hugh is 14 and his sister, Alice is 12.

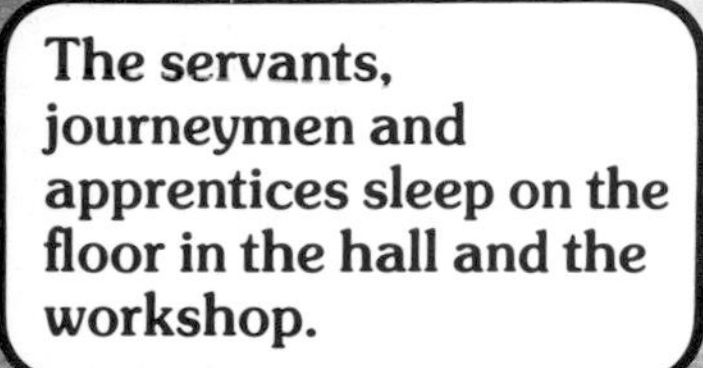

Here are some of the other people who live and work in the Middleton's house.

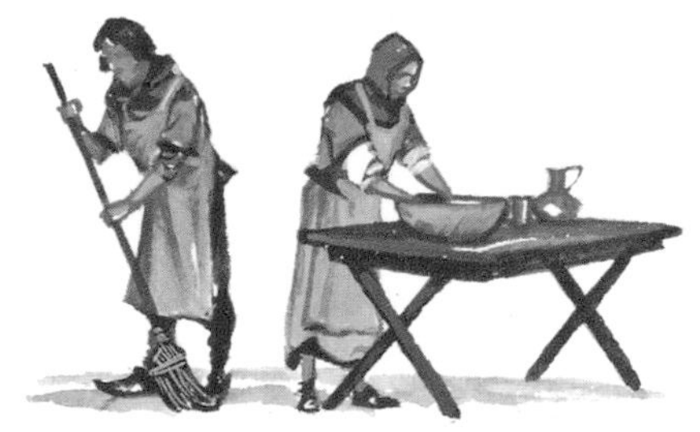

The maid, Nan, and her husband, Dick, do most of the cooking and cleaning.

The two journeymen*, Will and Walter, work for Master Middleton in his goldsmith's workshop.

Ned and Nick are both 14. They are Master Middleton's apprentices. They help in the workshop and are learning to be goldsmiths. They do not get paid.

**Journeymen are trained craftsmen who work for other people in return for wages.*

Getting up and going to school

Everyone gets up very early in the morning. In the winter it is still dark when Thomas wakes up.

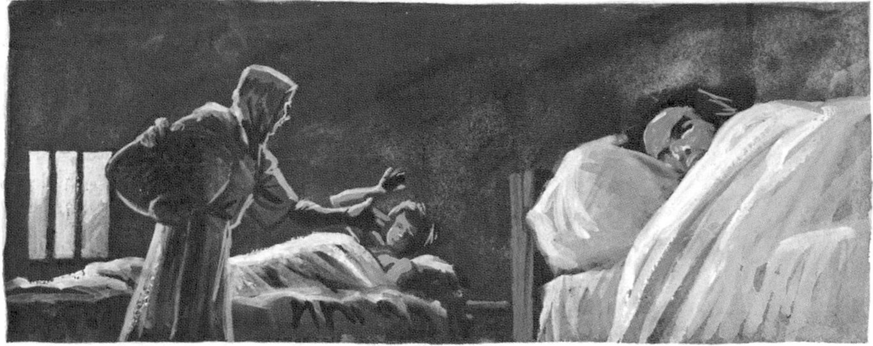

At five o'clock, Nan, the maid, comes into the room Thomas shares with his brother, Hugh. She brings a jug filled with cold water from a well in the garden.

She opens the wooden shutters that cover the window at night. Sometimes she has to shake the boys and splash them with water to wake them up.

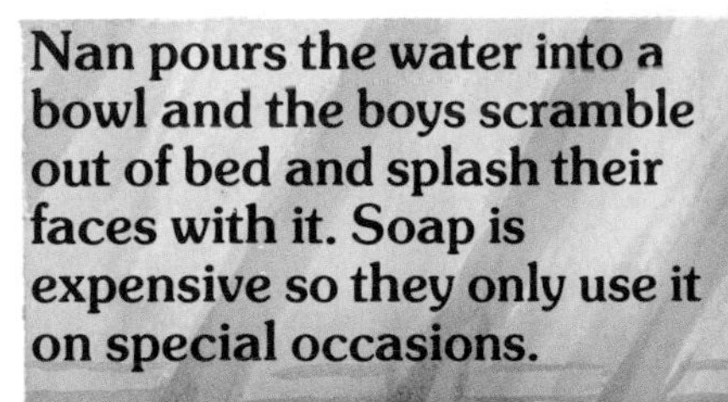

Nan pours the water into a bowl and the boys scramble out of bed and splash their faces with it. Soap is expensive so they only use it on special occasions.

On the way to school Thomas goes past the place where the new cathedral is being built. The workmen are already hard at work. Thomas loves to stand and watch them. He does not stay too long because he is frightened of being late for school.

As he hurries along, he usually passes Gilbert Star, the nightwatchman. Gilbert has patrolled the streets all night, making sure everything is peaceful.

Thomas fetches his clothes from a peg on the wall. He takes off his nightshirt and pulls on his thick woollen tunic and hose (tights) and his leather shoes.

There are no bathrooms or toilets inside the Middleton's house, but there is a toilet in a wooden shed, which has been built on to the side of the house.

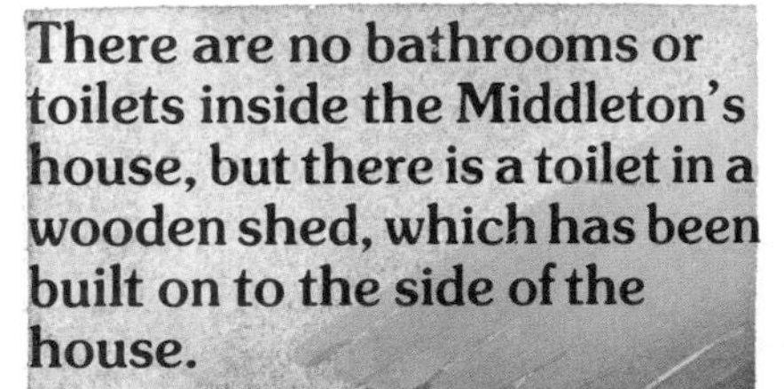

Thomas does not have much breakfast before he goes to school. He goes into the kitchen and grabs a hunk of bread and some cheese to eat on his way.

The street is already very busy. Thomas has to keep dodging out of the way of carts and packhorses. People from the countryside are bringing animals, vegetables and other food to sell in the markets and shops.

People throw all their rubbish out of their windows into the streets. They usually give a warning shout so you can jump out of the way, but it makes the streets very smelly.

At school

Thomas arrives at school just before the clock strikes six. It is next to St Peter's Church and is called St Peter's Grammar School. There are about 90 boys divided into three classes.

The master at the school is the priest at St Peter's Church. He has two assistants to help him teach. They are both training to be priests.

Books are very expensive because they have to be written by hand. Only the master has a book. It is made out of parchment (animal skin).

The boys write on slates covered with wax. The wax can be melted and smoothed, so the slate can be used lots of times.

All the lessons are in Latin and the boys are supposed to speak only Latin all the time they are at school. The master reads out passages from a book and the boys learn them by heart.

The master is very strict. If a boy does not learn his lesson well, he beats him with a bunch of sticks. He also beats them if they are late or forget to speak in Latin.

Alice's lessons

While Thomas is out at school, his sister, Alice, stays at home. First she helps her mother with all the things that need doing in the house, so that when she gets married she will know how to run her own house. Then she has some lessons.

▲ In the kitchen they check the stores of food and drink and decide what extra supplies they need to buy.

They collect herbs and flowers from the garden. Some of these they scatter on the floor in the house to make it smell nice. ▶

◀ They check that Nan has swept out all the rooms. The hall floor is covered with rushes to mop up food and dirt and these have to be changed once a week.

Alice's mother shows her how to crush herbs and use them with other ingredients to make medicines for the family. ▼

▲ Alice has already learnt how to sew. She helps with the clothes that need mending. She also decorates linen and wallhangings with elaborate embroidery.

Her mother is teaching her how to read and write. She does not enjoy it much, but her mother makes her practise every day. ▼

▲ When she has finished her writing lesson, her music tutor arrives. He teaches her how to play tunes on the instrument shown in this picture, which is called a psaltery. He also gives her singing lessons.

Going shopping

When she has finished her lessons, Alice often goes shopping with her mother.

All shops selling the same type of things are gathered together in one street.

Each shop has a painted picture sign to show what it sells, because most people cannot read.

The shops are very small. The shopkeepers keep their goods in the front part of their houses.

Alice and her mother are buying some cloth. They will take it to a tailor and ask him to make Alice a new dress.

Wooden shutters from the windows let down to make counters, which stick out into the street.

This is a barber's shop. The barber is about to give this man a shave.

This woman is selling fresh fruit from the countryside.

Hot pie seller

Beggar

People often carry bunches of herbs or flowers to smell, because the streets smell so filthy.

You have to watch out for thieves and pickpockets.

Nan, the maid, goes to the market to buy fresh meat and vegetables for dinner.

This butcher has been caught selling rotten meat. As a punishment he has been put in the pillory, where people throw rotten meat at him.

While his mother and sister are shopping, Thomas is on his way back from school. He takes the long way home, so he can watch people practising archery in the field below the castle.

When he arrives home he finds Ned and Nick playing ball in the street with some other apprentices. He joins in. The games are very rough and often end in fights. He hopes his father does not catch them playing.

Dinner Time

Dinner is at six o'clock in the Middleton's house. It is the main meal of the day. In the kitchen Nan and Dick are busy getting it ready. Mistress Middleton is making sure they do everything right.

The family drink wine out of pewter goblets. The children mix water with their wine.

Each person has a knife, a spoon and a plate. These are made of pewter (a mixture of tin and lead). There are no forks.

People throw their scraps and bones on the floor and the dogs eat them up.

Everyone who lives in the house eats together. Members of the family and guests sit at the top table. Servants, journeymen

Thomas is holding a basin of water for a guest at the top table. Everyone washes their hands and dries them on napkins.

Hugh carves the meat before passing it round.

The servants eat off wooden plates and drink beer from clay mugs.

Each person has a thick slice of bread to eat with their meat. There are no potatoes in Europe at this time.

and apprentices sit at the lower table. Before anyone sits down Master Middleton says a prayer.

After dinner Thomas and Alice play with their toys before going to bed.

Thomas has some toy soldiers made out of wood and string. When you pull the strings their arms and legs move.

Alice has a pet bird in a cage. Her father bought it for her the last time there was a fair in the town.

Hugh has a chess set. He is teaching Thomas how to play.

These are Alice's dolls. They have wooden heads and their bodies are made of cloth stuffed with straw.

Sometimes in the summer they play outside in the garden with wooden bats and balls.

In the workshop

Thomas's brother, Hugh, does not go to school anymore. He works in his father's workshop. One day he will take over the business from his father and run it all by himself.

In the workshop they make jewellery and jugs and plates for noblemen and churches. They work very hard every day except for Sundays.

Master Middleton is talking to the bishop of Castletown about some cups and plates he has ordered.

All the men in the town who work in a trade are members of a kind of club, called a guild. There is a different guild for every trade. This year Master Middleton was chosen as the leader of the Goldsmith's Guild. They meet in the Goldsmith's Hall and make rules that all the members have to obey.

In each guild there are master craftsmen, journeymen and apprentices. The apprentices of one guild often get into fights with apprentices from another guild or with students from the university.

Walter is decorating a gold cup with jewels.

Will is heating up gold in a small pot over the stove.

Hugh is pouring the liquid gold into moulds to make plates.

Nick is carving a pattern round the edge of a gold plate.

Every Easter there is a special festival. All the guilds put on plays. Each guild acts a different story from the Bible. The goldsmiths are doing the story of the three wise men. They do the plays in the street on wooden carts called pageants. People from all the nearby villages come to town to see the plays. Women are not allowed to belong to the guild, so boys take any women's parts.

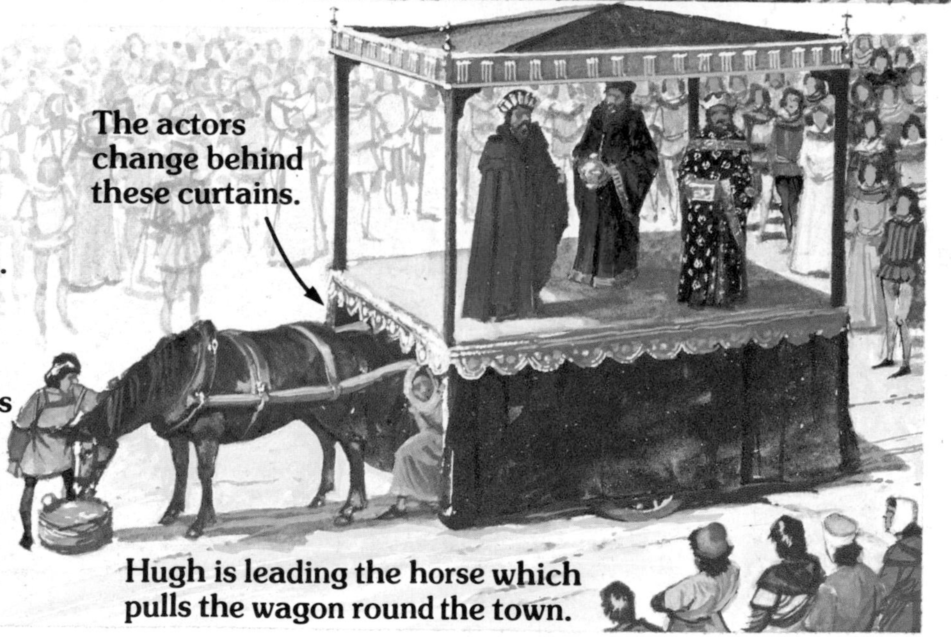

The actors change behind these curtains.

Hugh is leading the horse which pulls the wagon round the town.

Trip to a monastery

When Thomas is older he is going to work for his Uncle Roger, who is a wool merchant. Today he is setting off on a trip to the countryside to buy wool. Thomas is allowed to go with him.

Warehouse by the river where wool is stored.

They are taking several packhorses with them to carry the wool back to the town.

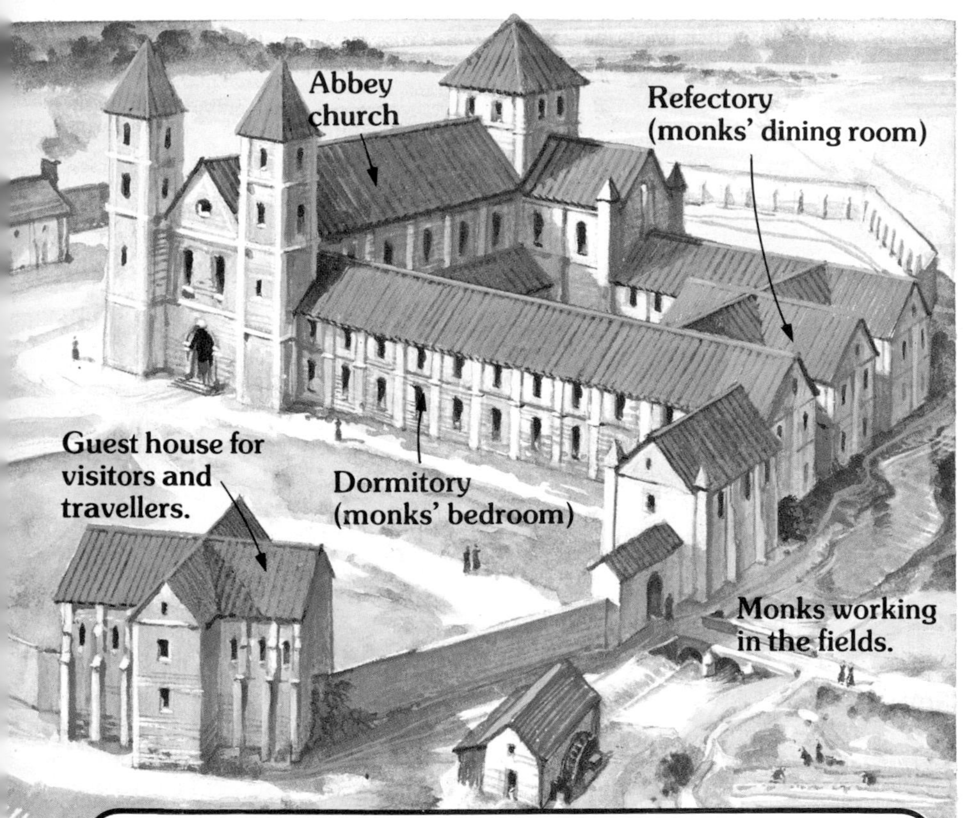

After a long day of riding along rough tracks they arrive at Farland Abbey. This is a monastery, where monks live and work together. Uncle Roger is going to buy wool from the monks.

The Abbot (the head of the monastery) meets them at the main gates. He takes them to the guest house, where they are going to stay the night. People travelling on long journeys often stay in the monks' guest house.

The next morning Uncle Roger buys the wool he wants and the servants load up the packhorses. Meanwhile, one of the monks takes Thomas to have a look round the monastery.

First they look inside the church. The monks spend a lot of time every day praying and singing here.

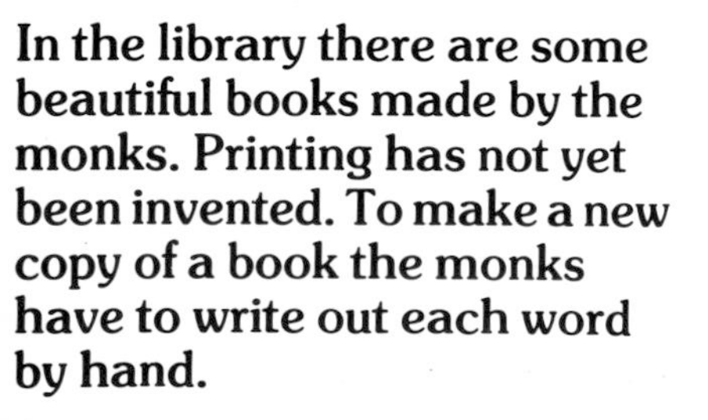

In the library there are some beautiful books made by the monks. Printing has not yet been invented. To make a new copy of a book the monks have to write out each word by hand.

The monks look after sick people in a special part of the monastery called the infirmary. They treat them with medicines made from herbs. There are hardly any hospitals at this time.

The monks also help poor people who have nowhere else to go. At the abbey gates they hand out left-over food and a small sum of money, known as a dole, to anyone they think deserves it.

Trip to a village

Thomas and Uncle Roger are arriving at the village of Longford. They are going to buy some more wool here before travelling home.

Tomorrow is the day of the Longford fair. People are travelling from far and wide to buy and sell things at the fair.

The fair starts as soon as it is light the next day. Many of the villagers are selling things they have grown or made. Merchants have brought all sorts of rare goods from distant places.

There are also jugglers, fortune-tellers and other entertainers. Uncle Roger is buying wool from the Lord of the Manor's bailiff (the man who manages all the lord's land and property).

They arrive at the village inn just as a party of pilgrims ride up. They are on their way to a holy place to show their devotion to God. The inn is very crowded so some of them will have to sleep on the floor.

They all have supper in the inn together and Thomas enjoys hearing the stories about things that have happened to the pilgrims on their journey. They have already been travelling for several weeks.

Inside the castle

Today Master Middleton is going to visit Lord John in his castle. Hugh and Thomas are going with their father. Master Middleton is going to arrange for his daughter, Alice, to be married to Lord John's son, Henry.

The guards are expecting them and pull up the portcullis to let them through the gate. In the courtyard servants hurry forward to hold their horses' heads, while they dismount. Lord John and Henry come forward to greet them.

Lord John takes Master Middleton to the great hall to discuss the marriage. Master Middleton promises to provide a large dowry (sum of money) with Alice, when the marriage takes place. They agree that Alice and Henry are too young to be married for a few years yet, but decide to celebrate their engagement with a tournament and banquet.

While their fathers are busy, Henry takes Hugh and Thomas to have a look round the castle. They have never been inside it before. Here he is leading them up a spiral staircase to the battlements.

At the top of the staircase the boys come out on an open walk which runs right round the castle walls. Soldiers, armed with bows and arrows and pikes, keep watch day and night.

They go back down to the very bottom of the staircase and arrive at the castle dungeons. Here outlaws who have robbed and killed people on Lord John's lands are kept chained to the walls.

Next Henry takes them to see the armourer's workshop. The armourer and his assistants make and repair all the bows, arrows, pikes, swords and armour for the soldiers who guard the castle.

Then they go to the stables. Lord John has several horses for himself and his family and each knight who lives in the castle has his own horse. Next door to the stables are the kennels. Here the hunting dogs are kept.

Falcons for hunting are kept in buildings called mews. They are used for catching other birds and small animals. Lord John and his followers spend a lot of time out hunting. Sometimes they catch deer and wild boars.

Alice's engagement

On the day of the engagement, Alice and her mother are carried to the castle in a litter. Master Middleton and the boys ride in front. Everyone is wearing their best clothes and Alice has a new dress on.

In the great hall of the castle Lord John and Master Middleton sign documents containing all the details of the marriage agreement. Then Alice and Henry give each other rings.

The area where the fight takes place is called the lists.

Crests on their helmets help people to tell which knight is which.

A wooden barrier called the tilt stops the horses crashing into each other.

To celebrate the engagement a tournament is held in the field below the castle wall. The guests watch from covered stands while knights on horseback charge at each other with long lances and try to knock each other to the ground.

Henry is not a knight yet. He is still a squire, whose job is to serve a knight. When he is older his father will knight him and he will be called Sir Henry. When he marries Alice, she will become Lady Alice.

After the tournament everyone goes back to the castle for a magnificent banquet. It is held in the great hall and will last for several hours. The Middletons sit with Lord John's family on the high table.

Pages and squires wait on the knights

Musicians play in the minstrels' gallery.

Index